The LAIRD'S Return

A HIGHLAND
FESTIVE
ROMANCE
NOVELLA

JAYNE CASTEL

WINTER MIST
PRESS

Is it too late for a second chance at love? An embittered laird. A loyal wife. A new start. A Yuletide romance in Medieval Scotland.

Robert De Keith has spent the last eight years rotting in an English dungeon. But when he returns home to Dunnottar Castle, he soon realizes he doesn't fit into his old life anymore.

His wife, Elizabeth, has ruled the castle in his absence. However, the woman who greets him now seems a stranger. Time and events have altered them both.

As Yule approaches, Robert and Elizabeth struggle to salvage their marriage and overcome the bitterness and distrust that separates them. But can they—or has life changed them both too much?

THE LAIRD'S RETURN is a stand-alone Highland Festive Novella about the power of enduring love set in the same world as THE IMMORTAL HIGHLAND CENTURIONS.

Historical Romances
by Jayne Castel

DARK AGES BRITAIN

The Kingdom of the East Angles series
Night Shadows (prequel novella)
Dark Under the Cover of Night (Book One)
Nightfall till Daybreak (Book Two)
The Deepening Night (Book Three)
The Kingdom of the East Angles: The Complete Series

The Kingdom of Mercia series
The Breaking Dawn (Book One)
Darkest before Dawn (Book Two)
Dawn of Wolves (Book Three)
The Kingdom of Mercia: The Complete Series

The Kingdom of Northumbria series
The Whispering Wind (Book One)
Wind Song (Book Two)
Lord of the North Wind (Book Three)
The Kingdom of Northumbria: The Complete Series

DARK AGES SCOTLAND

The Warrior Brothers of Skye series
Blood Feud (Book One)
Barbarian Slave (Book Two)
Battle Eagle (Book Three)
The Warrior Brothers of Skye: The Complete Series

The Pict Wars series
Warrior's Heart (Book One)
Warrior's Secret (Book Two)
Warrior's Wrath (Book Three)
The Pict Wars: The Complete Series

Novellas
Winter's Promise

MEDIEVAL SCOTLAND

The Brides of Skye series
The Beast's Bride (Book One)
The Outlaw's Bride (Book Two)
The Rogue's Bride (Book Three)
The Brides of Skye: The Complete Series

The Sisters of Kilbride series
Unforgotten (Book One)
Awoken (Book Two)
Fallen (Book Three)
Claimed (Epilogue novella)

The Immortal Highland Centurions series
Maximus (Book One)
Cassian (Book Two)
Draco (Book Three)
The Laird's Return (Epilogue festive novella)

Epic Fantasy Romances by Jayne Castel

Light and Darkness series
Ruled by Shadows (Book One)
The Lost Swallow (Book Two)
Path of the Dark (Book Three)
Light and Darkness: The Complete Series

***

To my readers!

***

*"It's not what they take away from you that counts.
It's what you do with what you have left.*
—Hubert Humphrey

I

THE IMPOSTER

Dunnottar Castle
Scotland
Winter, 1308

HIS FEET AND hands were numb by the time Dunnottar rose against the northern sky.

Robert De Keith drew up his sturdy garron, his gaze taking in the view before him.

How often over the past eight years had he dreamed of this moment? There had been times when he'd despaired, when he'd believed he'd never see home again, never set foot on Scottish soil once more.

Robert blinked, dislodging a snow flake that had settled on his eyelashes. Around him, white blanketed the world in a chill crust. His garron stood up to its fetlocks in snow. Winter held Scotland in its grip as the 'Long Night' approached. Yuletide was just a few days away now.

Remaining there, staring at the grey curtain walls, Robert felt as if he'd strayed into a dream. It had been a long journey up from Warkworth Castle in Northumberland—where he'd been imprisoned for nearly a decade. Even when they'd let him walk free, he'd had difficulty believing it.

He'd expected to feel joy at seeing Dunnottar again—but, strangely, he didn't.

Instead, he felt nothing.

Urging the garron forward, Robert rode toward the cliff-top opposite the castle. Dunnottar held a strategically defensive position upon a rocky outcrop, linked to the mainland by a thin strip of land. The approach was difficult—much to the chagrin of those who'd attempted to lay siege to the castle over the years. A steep path led down from the gates to the bottom of the cliff on which Robert now dismounted his garron.

Carefully, he led his mount down the slope, testing each step. Under normal circumstances this slope was tricky, but covered with snow it was perilous. Robert didn't want his faithful mount to break a leg.

Reaching the bottom, Robert swung up onto the garron's back once more and urged the stout pony up to the gates. Craning his neck, he spied the outlines of men wielding spears silhouetted against the pale sky and fluttering snow.

"Who goes there?" One of the guards shouted. "What's yer business at Dunnottar, stranger?"

Robert's mouth twisted into a bitter smile. *Stranger?*

Aye, he'd been gone long enough now that his own men wouldn't recognize him these days. Frankly, despite that this magnificent keep belonged to him, he didn't feel comfortable returning.

Shoving aside the sensation, Robert peered up at the helmed face above him. "I'm Robert De Keith," he called back, his voice ringing off stone. "Laird of this castle. Open the gates!"

The Captain of the Dunnottar Guard met Robert in the lower ward bailey.

Cassian Gaius's face split into a wide grin as he strode across the snow-covered cobbles to meet him. A cloak of De Keith plaid—blue, green, and turquoise cross-hatchings—rippled from his shoulders. "Robert! You're alive."

The welcome, although warm, made tension ripple through Robert.

So, they all think I'm dead?

Once again, a sensation of displacement flooded over him. He didn't belong here. He was an interloper, a man who'd risen from the dead.

"I am." Robert managed a tight smile. None of this was Cassian's fault. He'd always liked the Spaniard—an enigmatic warrior who'd joined the Dunnottar Guard a few years before Robert's capture and proved himself worthy of leading it within the turning of a year.

As the captain neared, Robert noted that he looked older: his skin was a little more leathery, and there were laughter lines around the eyes. However, his brown hair, slightly longer than Robert remembered, was still untouched by silver.

Aye, we're all older. Robert was sure he too had been weathered by the passing of time. *Have the years been kind to Elizabeth?*

The thought brought Robert up short, his gaze flicking to the keep towering above him. The numbness in his chest disappeared then, replaced by a squeezing sensation.

Was his wife even here? Nearly a decade had passed since his capture. If she, like Cassian, thought he was dead, she may have returned to her kin.

"Captain." Robert dismounted the Highland pony and strode to the big man. They clasped arms, and for the first time since leaving Warkworth, Robert felt a flicker of warmth within him.

The joy on the captain's face wasn't feigned. Cassian's eyes gleamed, his gaze riveted upon Robert. "So, those bastards finally let you go?"

Robert nodded, his mouth thinning. His release had been a shock to him too. He'd dreaded the day his captors would take him from the cells and to the walls, where they'd string him up on the gallows.

Years had inched by as he waited for the day to come. But it hadn't.

"So, David's gotten comfortable in my chair, has he?" Robert cocked an eyebrow. It was better if he kept this exchange light, even if his gut was now tying itself up in knots.

He wasn't looking forward to seeing David. His brother had always coveted power and wouldn't want to relinquish his position.

The captain grew still, his hazel eyes narrowing. "You don't know about David?"

Robert frowned, the tension within him winding tighter. "I've been locked up in an English dungeon for years, Gaius," he growled. "Not one missive from Dunnottar reached me in that time. How would I know what has befallen my brother?"

Cassian's expression grew grave. "He's dead, Robert. Seven years ago now."

Silence fell between them while Robert took in this news. He wasn't going to feign grief. David had been a weasel, and likely hadn't made the slightest effort to get his elder brother returned.

Even so, he hadn't expected this.

"How?" he asked finally.

Cassian cleared his throat. "Well ... that's quite a tale, De Keith." He paused then, dragging a hand through his shaggy hair. "He tried to kill Edward Longshanks and got a dirk to the throat for his trouble."

Robert sucked in a surprised breath. "What?"

Cassian's mouth twisted. "I know ... hard to believe, but true. Go up and see Lady Elizabeth ... I'm sure she'll fill you in on all the details."

So, she's still at Dunnottar after all.

Robert's pulse started to race. The mention of Elizabeth was a jab to the belly. He wasn't ready to face her again, not yet.

Coward.

This was what he wanted, wasn't it? All he'd thought about for many years was his wife. The promise of being reunited with her was the only thing that had kept him going. But when he didn't hear from her, despair had slowly descended upon him. Anger followed, till an ember of resentment glowed hot in his belly. For the last months, he'd felt torn whenever thoughts of Elizabeth crept into his mind.

And now that he stood within Dunnottar's lower ward bailey—laird of his lands once more—longing warred with bitterness and anger.

Aye, Elizabeth hadn't returned to her kin. All the same, she likely thought herself a widow these days. How would she feel about having her husband return from the dead? He felt like an imposter—but would she treat him like one?

Robert cleared his throat, his heart now pounding—and despite the chill day and the snow that continued to fall silently around him, he was sweating. When he spoke, his voice held a hoarse edge. "Elizabeth ... is she well?"

Cassian smiled. "She is. Lady Elizabeth has been laird of Dunnottar in your absence."

II

AN AWKWARD REUNION

"ELIZABETH! YER HUSBAND is here!"

The words, which Gavina cried as she burst into the solar, made Elizabeth stab herself in the finger.

Dropping both the needle and her embroidery, Elizabeth stared—dumbstruck—at the heavily pregnant woman before her.

Gavina's belly had grown huge over the past fortnight. Elizabeth was sure the birth was just days away now. Gavina had actually started to waddle as she walked.

But Elizabeth paid none of that any attention at present—instead, she stared at Gavina as if she'd just announced a troupe of brownies had flooded into the keep.

"What did ye just say?" The question came out in a strangled gasp.

"Robert!" Gavina clasped her hands over her swollen belly. "He's returned!"

Elizabeth rose to her feet, her embroidery fluttering to the floor. Her heart started to thud painfully against her breast bone, and she suddenly felt light-headed. "Where is he?"

"On his way up to see ye."

Elizabeth stared at Gavina a moment longer.

Robert's here?

Rousing herself, she shot past her friend, her feet moving of their own accord.

Joy filtered up as the shock abated. For years, she'd believed him dead—that King Edward of England had ordered him executed after what her brother-by-marriage had done.

But Gavina wasn't lying. She'd seen the truth in the woman's eyes.

Robert was alive and had returned to Dunnottar.

Picking up her skirts, Elizabeth practically flew down the hallway, past the chamber where Father Finlay was teaching Robbie Latin—she could hear their voices as the lad recited words after the chaplain.

But Elizabeth didn't alter her course, didn't halt to take her son from his lessons.

She had to see this first. She had to witness Robert with her own eyes before she'd believe he'd survived.

They met halfway down the stairs.

Elizabeth halted, her gaze alighting upon a tall, broad-shouldered man with long brown hair, who came to a stop a few steps below her.

For a moment, they just stared at each other.

Elizabeth drank him in.

Robert was both unchanged, and yet different.

He had the same flowing hair and short beard, the same piercing brown eyes. Clad in a mail shirt and thick leather braies, a heavy fur mantle about his shoulders, he was every inch the warrior she remembered. Yet his face was altered—thinner, more careworn, his eyes hollowed from fatigue. There were also flecks of silver in his hair and beard that hadn't been there years earlier.

Robert stared up at her, his gaze as searing as she remembered. Yet he didn't smile, didn't exclaim at the sight of her.

Pushing aside the uneasiness that stole over her, Elizabeth drew in a sharp breath, gathering her courage.

Goose ... he's yer husband. What do ye have to be nervous about?

And yet she was.

"Robert," she murmured his name—and then she moved, taking the next few steps toward him, while he did the same, alighting the last steps till they collided.

Elizabeth's breathing caught as his arms went about her. Clasping him close, she realized that underneath his mail shirt, leather vest, and lèine, he was as lean and wiry as a hunting hound.

The man she'd seen off that fateful day over eight years earlier had been broad and muscular. The English clearly had been starving him.

Tears welled, hot and stinging, and Elizabeth's vision blurred. She squeezed him tight, as if to make sure he was real and not merely a figment of her imagination.

Her voice came out in a whisper. "Rob ... is it really ye?"

"Aye, Liz." That voice—how she'd missed it, dreamed of it. The low timbre, the slight gravelly edge. It had haunted her dreams. "Ye still smell of lilies."

Elizabeth smiled through her tears. She'd always worn oil perfumed with the scented leaves of lily—a perfume she remembered Robert loving.

All those years ago, when they'd been young and carefree.

Drawing back, Elizabeth brushed away her tears and raised her chin to meet her husband's gaze.

He stared down at her, a strange, almost pained expression upon his face. "Ye haven't changed at all," he murmured. Did she imagine it, or was there a note of reserve in his voice? "Whereas, I fear I'm not the man ye remember."

"Nonsense," she scoffed, even if the look he was giving her put Elizabeth on edge. It wasn't true she hadn't changed. Whenever she caught a glimpse of her reflection these days in the looking glass, she thought how tired she looked. "Ye are thinner than I remember," she continued, nervousness making her tongue run away with her, "but just as handsome." Elizabeth stepped back from him. She wanted to catch his hand, entwine her fingers through his, but suddenly felt too nervous to do so. "Come up to the solar, and I'll have some supper brought up to ye."

The crackling hearth cast a warm glow over the laird's solar. A large lump of peat burned there. It gradually warmed Robert's chilled limbs, his numbed fingers and toes.

Sighing, Robert reached for the cup of wine at his elbow before meeting the eye of the woman seated across the table from him. "That," he said with the barest hint of a smile, "was the best thing I've ever eaten."

Elizabeth smiled, and he found himself staring at her full lips and the dimple on her right cheek. "I recall that pottage and oaten dumplings were always a favorite of yers," she replied.

"Aye." Robert took a gulp from his cup. "As is bramble wine."

"It was a good year for brambles," she replied, still smiling, although her midnight-blue eyes had a guarded, watchful look to them. "The hedgerows were overflowing this year. We had brambles with every meal for weeks … they're Robbie's favorite."

Elizabeth halted here—it was the first time she'd mentioned their son. Since they'd come upstairs to the solar, the pair of them had spoken of inconsequential things—the weather, Yuletide preparations, and their meal.

It was as if they were strangers.

Robert had deliberately kept her at arm's length since their meeting in the stairwell. Even if seeing her again had stripped him of breath.

Robert lowered his cup, his gaze taking his wife in. When he'd told her she'd barely altered, he'd meant it. Truthfully though, the woman was even more beautiful than he remembered. She wore her thick dark-blonde hair unbound, and the dark-blue kirtle she wore suited her coloring, accentuating the loveliness of her skin and the brightness of her eyes. It also highlighted the lush curves of her body, curves that were perhaps more generous than he remembered, but only added to her loveliness.

Eight years had passed since he'd seen this woman— and his gaze couldn't get enough of her.

And yet, he held himself in check. He couldn't bring himself to tell her how much he'd missed her—how it was thoughts of her that kept him going over the years, before hope had turned to ashes.

Instead, his voice was cool and detached when he finally asked, "And how is Robbie?"

"Growing faster than a weed," Elizabeth replied, smiling once more. And yet once again, Robert noted the reserve in her eyes. "He just had his tenth birthday."

"The fifteenth of December," Robert murmured.

Elizabeth's gaze widened. "Ye remember?"

He inclined his head. "Of course."

Elizabeth cleared her throat, while Robert took another sip of wine. God's teeth, it was awkward between them, and he couldn't seem to find the words to ease things.

"Cassian told me how David died," he said after a lengthy pause. "But he said ye'd fill me in on the rest."

Her full mouth thinned. "It happened in 1301," she confirmed. "While Edward Longshanks held Stirling, yer brother went there with the purpose of bending the knee."

Robert scowled. "What?" His brother had been a snake, but he hadn't thought he'd kiss Longshanks's arse.

"It was a ruse," Elizabeth assured him hurriedly. "Wallace was in hiding here at the time, and he wanted to know what Longshanks was planning … and I wanted to make a plea for yer life."

Robert went still. During his lost years at Warkworth, the only news from the world beyond that had reached him was the death of William Wallace. His guards had crowed over it. Discovering now that Wallace had been sheltering at Dunnottar wasn't hugely surprising—after all, the freedom fighter had once liberated the stronghold. Instead, he focused on the fact his wife had spoken directly to Edward of England on his behalf. "Ye did?"

Elizabeth frowned. "Ye sound surprised," she observed. "Did ye think I'd just leave things as they were?"

Robert took a sip of wine, in an attempt to mask the discomfort that now washed over him. Aye, in the end he had. "I was locked away for a long while, Liz," he said after a moment. "When the years passed and I didn't hear from ye ... I thought ye'd moved on."

Silence fell between them then, broken only by the crackling of the hearth.

"Longshanks agreed to send ye a missive from me," Elizabeth said stiffly. Hurt flickered across her face. "But after David's assassination attempt, I imagine he set fire to it."

Her words hung between them.

The knowledge that his wife had pleaded to Edward to deliver word to him should have brought Robert solace, but instead the urge to accuse her of giving up on him writhed within him. That incident was years ago. Had she never tried again?

Although she'd greeted him warmly, Robert had seen the shock in his wife's eyes, followed by an uncharacteristic reserve.

He was a ghost from her past.

Robert's throat constricted. Once again, he felt as if he was intruding. His wife hadn't exactly been pining for him. Before he'd entered the keep earlier, Cassian had been full of praise for how well she'd ruled Dunnottar since David's death.

"It's nearing Robbie's bedtime, but would ye like to see him first?" Elizabeth broke the brittle tension between them by wisely changing the subject.

Robert shook his head, weariness descending upon him. He wasn't ready to see his son. Robbie had been halfway through his second summer when Robert had been captured—barely more than a bairn. His conversation with Elizabeth had shredded his nerves; he didn't want another reunion tonight.

He suddenly felt bone-tired—as if he could sleep for a week. He was sore, both of heart and spirit, and just wanted to crawl away and lick his wounds.

"Not tonight," he replied, downing the last of the wine.

III

SEPARATE CHAMBERS

ELIZABETH TENSED, HER fingers curling around the cup of wine she'd barely touched.

The man opposite her—the husband she'd longed for to the point of pain over the years—had just refused to greet his child.

His son.

For a moment, she merely stared at him, waiting for him to rethink his decision.

But when he didn't, anger quickened in her breast.

"Robbie has indeed grown while ye were away," she said, her voice turning cold. "He was barely more than a babe when ye left ... and is now almost the same height as me."

Robert tensed, his gaze shuttering. And when he replied, his tone was also wintry. "Ye speak as if I've been away on Crusade, Liz." His gaze fused with hers. "I didn't 'leave'. I was captured." A nerve flickered in his cheek, before he put down the pewter goblet he was holding with a 'thud'. "The lad has gotten used to living without a father. One more night won't make a difference."

Elizabeth sucked in an angry breath, heat flushing through her. The man she remembered had been proud and arrogant—a warrior to the core—but he'd also been warm, with a ready smile. Before his capture, Robert De Keith had readily shown affection for his wife and son.

Elizabeth didn't recognize the man before her now. He was so cold, so distant.

Her throat constricted. His behavior reminded her of the argument they'd had before he left Dunnottar years earlier. She hadn't wanted him to go on that campaign. The urge to broach the subject bubbled up inside her, yet she swallowed it. Tonight wasn't the right time for such a conversation.

Robert then dragged a tired hand down his face. "I'm exhausted," he muttered. "I shall withdraw to my chamber."

Elizabeth went still. She'd noted the inflection on the word 'my'. He was retiring for the evening—alone.

The laird and lady of Dunnottar had always had separate quarters, each with a solar, dressing chamber, and bed-chamber. Elizabeth's chambers looked south over the coast and the sea, while Robert's held a commanding view of the cliff-top and green hills to the west. But before his departure, Robert had spent his nights in his wife's bed-chamber. They'd rarely slept apart.

A chill settled in the pit of Elizabeth's belly, dousing her anger. Her joy at seeing her husband alive and well faded as she realized they weren't going to be able to pick up where they left off.

There was a high curtain wall between them now. One Elizabeth had no idea how to scale.

Robert reminded her of his younger brother tonight. David De Keith's scornful attitude to the women in his life had always angered Elizabeth. During his six-year marriage to Gavina—who was now happily wed to Draco, and pregnant with their third child—Elizabeth had hardly ever seen him treat his wife with anything but scorn.

Robert had always been so different, and just a little part of her had been smug at how fortunate she had been. Like most well-born Scottish lasses, she'd had little choice in her husband—but she'd found happiness with Robert De Keith.

Before his capture, he'd been devoted to her.

Silence hung between them now, and when Elizabeth didn't answer, Robert rose to his feet. "Goodnight, Liz."

He didn't move across to her, didn't favor her with a smile or a kiss on the cheek.

Instead, he crossed the wide solar and disappeared, the door closing softly behind him.

Robert stood before the hearth in his bed-chamber, his gaze upon the large lump of peat that glowed there.

His chamber was exactly as he remembered it—a large space with deerskins covering the cold flagstones and a huge bed draped in fine blankets and furs in the center. The room was largely unadorned. There was only a table by the bed, where a bank of candles burned and a wash bowl sat. The stone walls were plain, save for the huge claidheamh-mòr hanging opposite the bed. Robert turned from the fire, his attention settling now upon the weapon.

His father's sword. The great blade had a nick in it, the result of an axe blow during one of the many battles his father had fought in.

Robert's mouth curved in a humorless smile. He came from a long line of warriors. Sometimes it seemed as if he'd come out of the womb fighting.

Tonight he felt drained by it all—by life itself.

Turning back to the fire, he began to undress, unfastening his mail shirt and unbuckling his belt.

He'd offended Elizabeth.

A sigh gusted out of him as he recalled how her dark-blue eyes had narrowed, her beautiful mouth flattening. She'd always been strong-willed, yet tonight he didn't have the energy to spar with her.

And nor had he the energy to meet his son.

Ten winters old.

In a few years, the lad he remembered as a toddling bairn would be a man.

Another warrior who would one day take his father's place as laird.

Robert draped his clothing over the back of a chair and padded naked to the bed. A groan escaped him as he slid under the blankets. It had been a long while since he'd slept in a bed, let alone one as comfortable as this.

His narrow cot in his cell at Warkworth had been better than the damp stone floor many prisoners had to deal with. Even so, it had been an uncomfortable bed, with rough, scratchy blankets. And then, there had been unwelcome bed-fellows: the spiders and rodents who'd sometimes crawled onto the cot while he slept.

In comparison, this bed was paradise.

The only thing missing was a woman's warm body.

Robert stared up at the rafters, his thoughts turning back to Elizabeth. She was truly lovely to behold—bright sunshine after a long, bleak winter.

But he'd seen the chagrin in her eyes when he'd announced he was going to bed—alone.

She likely remembered that he'd always preferred her chamber. The air in that room was always warm and lightly scented with lavender. Colorful tapestries covered the walls, and soft cushions lay scattered about. Robert wondered if the space had changed over the years.

Perhaps not, but Elizabeth had. She'd grown more confident, competent. She had gotten on with her life, as she should have. He knew he shouldn't judge her for doing so, and yet he found that resentment still smoldered in his gut.

He'd changed too—had turned into a bitter individual who couldn't even feel joy at being reunited with his family. Right now, he was disgusted with himself.

It's not her fault. Robert clenched his jaw. *I'm not the man I was. Perhaps I should have done everyone a favor and stayed away.*

Nonetheless, he'd returned home, and that meant facing his wife. Given time, he would seek to ease the tension between them, even if he wasn't sure where to start.

Elizabeth felt oddly tearful as she readied herself for bed. Her maid, Morag, had helped her undress and was now brushing her hair in long, hard strokes.

Gritting her teeth as the hog-bristle brush caught on a knot, Elizabeth blinked rapidly, glad that her maid's roughness distracted her from the tightness in her throat and her blurring vision.

What a bitter disappointment this evening had been.

She'd been giddy with excitement earlier, asking the cooks to prepare supper for the laird; fortunately, there had been left-over pottage from the nooning meal. She'd also dressed carefully, in her finest blue kirtle that matched her eyes.

He didn't even notice.

Not that it mattered though—for the general awkwardness between them made the effort she'd made seem foolish and vain.

"That's it, My Lady," Morag announced. "Yer hair is done."

"Thank ye," Elizabeth replied, cursing the husky edge to her voice.

"Will that be all, My Lady?"

"Aye."

Morag was a dour older woman who'd served Elizabeth for years now—after her previous maid, Jean, met an unfortunate end. The lass, who'd secretly been David De Keith's lover, had died on the journey back from Stirling. They'd been fleeing for their lives after David had tried to assassinate the English king.

Adjusting the lace that did up the neck of her night-rail, Elizabeth rose from the stool and crossed to the hearth, letting the warmth seep through the thin material. Behind her, she heard Morag shuffle from the room.

She couldn't believe how badly her conversation with Robert had gone.

First he'd all but accused her of not caring what happened to him, then he'd refused to say goodnight to his son. And to complete things, he'd gone off to his own bed rather than sharing hers.

She'd been angry afterward, but now that she was alone, Elizabeth's throat constricted, despair welling within her. Perhaps it was best they slept apart now—for she wasn't sure she could weather more awkwardness between them.

What had happened to her loving husband, the man who used to tease her, his brown eyes gleaming with mischief?

She didn't recognize the cold stranger who'd returned to her.

A tear escaped, trickling down Elizabeth's face. *What did the English do to him?*

IV

SPARRING

ROBERT STEPPED OUT into the lower ward bailey and drew in a deep breath of gelid, salt-laced air.

The smell of Dunnottar, how he'd missed it over the years. The stench of Warkworth dungeons still lingered in his nostrils. He wondered if memories of the place would ever fade.

The cold bit into the exposed skin of his face—yet Robert welcomed it. He'd spent too many years trapped indoors, the world beyond limited to the tiny window high above.

Wrapping his fur mantle around himself, Robert crunched through the snow, past the stables on the right and the chapel on the left, to the blacksmith's forge that lay against the eastern walls. The castle's steward, Donnan De Keith, had let him know his son would be there this morning, helping the smith.

A frown creased Robert's brow as he approached the forge. His father would have smacked him around the head for spending time with the castle's smith.

A laird's son had better things to do with his time.

The clang of a hammer greeted him. Robert ducked inside to find a burly young man bent over an anvil, hammering out a sword-blade. Behind him was a lanky lad clad in leather braies and vest. The boy had his back to him.

Neither of them had yet noticed the laird's arrival, and so Robert observed his son for a few moments.

Elizabeth was right, the lad was growing like a weed. Robert had been like that at the same age—all long, gangly limbs—before his body filled out with muscle.

A mane of light brown hair fell over his shoulders as he finished stoking the forge and straightened up. Turning to speak to the smith, the lad suddenly realized they were no longer alone.

A face that was far more like Elizabeth's than his own stared back at him. The lad had De Keith eyes though: the color of weathered oak.

Robert stilled, and the same misgiving that had surfaced earlier that morning, when he'd told himself he needed to seek out his son, revisited him once more.

He had no idea what to say to this lad.

The blacksmith glanced up then, his gaze widening. "De Keith?"

Robert met his frank gaze. Of course, this man hadn't been smith when he'd last lived here. Blair Galbraith had worked this forge then—an ill-tempered brute but highly skilled all the same.

Robert had been shocked when Donnan told him that Galbraith had betrayed them all seven years earlier by informing Longshanks that the Wallace was sheltering at Dunnottar. A siege had followed, but fortunately the English king had been called away by an uprising to the south, sparing the fortress.

Struck dumb momentarily by the tale, and irritated that Elizabeth hadn't informed him of these events the night before, Robert had eventually asked the steward if Galbraith had ever paid for his treachery. He had. Word had reached the castle a year after Edward's siege that Comyn had sent men to Fintry to deal with Blair Galbraith. He'd not lived long enough to savor his vengeance upon the De Keiths.

Robert pushed aside thoughts of everything he'd missed in the past years and favored the smith with a tight smile. "Ye must be Connell?"

"Aye ... pleased to finally meet ye," the man replied with a grin. He then gestured to the lad behind him.

"Someone's been looking forward to seeing his Da again."

Robbie shot Connell a frown, clearly not appreciating the comment, before he straightened up properly, squaring his shoulders. "Morning, father."

How strange that word sounded.

"Father?" Robert quirked an eyebrow. "Since when did the De Keith's start talking like Englishmen? I'm yer 'Da', lad."

Robbie flushed, while Connell chuckled. "He's been a wee bit nervous, De Keith."

Robert nodded, before he stepped back, gesturing for his son to follow. He couldn't have a proper reunion with Robbie with Connell's commentary. His son's cheeks were glowing like twin embers now.

Robert walked out onto the lower ward, his boots sinking into powdery snow. Above him, the sky was pale, the glow of the winter sun barely visible. Another snowfall was on its way.

Robbie emerged, his face still burning. His expression was guarded, although Robert didn't blame him: the pair of them were strangers.

"Walk with me, lad," Robert grunted. "Let's go up to the walls." They crossed the bailey, passing the steps to the chapel and taking the postern door that led up to the upper ward.

The air was even colder up on the walls, yet Robert was too distracted to notice. He felt oddly uncomfortable in this lad's presence. He wasn't sure what to say to him. For years, he'd held onto an image of Robbie as an apple-cheeked bairn. Was this lanky boy with messy brown hair and a wary expression really his son?

Robert stopped before the southern ramparts, his gaze sweeping over the snow-clad hills, the frosted cliffs, and the grey North Sea.

"It's a grand view," he murmured, "and one I thought I'd never see again."

"It's good to have ye home, fa—Da ..." Robbie replied.

Robert tore his attention from the sweeping panorama, taking in his son once more. "A laird's son shouldn't be working in a forge, Robbie."

The lad's jaw tightened. "Ma doesn't mind. She says the work is good for me ... it builds muscle."

Robert snorted. "Sword practice and wrestling make a lad strong too," he replied. "They'll also prepare ye for the day ye'll have to fight yer first battle. Knowing how to hammer out a blade won't be much use to ye then."

Father and son locked gazes, and Robert saw how Robbie's jaw firmed, his spine growing stiff. The lad might have been nervous about seeing him again, yet he wasn't a coward. Robert flashed him a smile. "I'm keen to see how well ye wield a sword, lad," he continued. "Go fetch two wooden blades, and let's have a fight."

The "clack, clack" of wooden swords greeted Elizabeth when she emerged from the keep.

The morning drew out, and the noon meal approached. She hadn't seen her son or husband since dawn. She'd finally sought out Donnan, and the steward had told her that Robert had gone out to see Robbie in the forge.

Warmth had rushed through her chest at the news. Robert had clearly considered his rudeness the evening before and wanted to rectify matters.

However, when she stepped outdoors into the fluttering snow, her gaze traveling to two figures stripped to lèines and braies, the warmth faded.

Clack. Clack. Clack.

Robert was baring down on his son, face set in grim lines, as if the lad was a foe to be vanquished. Robbie—as game as ever—fought back. However, he wasn't a match for his father. He staggered back now, his left foot sliding in the snow as he struggled to keep his feet.

The duel had attracted a crowd. Captain Cassian Gaius stood a few yards away, his friend Draco next to him. Both men wore inscrutable expressions as they watched father and son fight. A few other men nearby were calling out encouragement to Robbie.

Elizabeth's pulse quickened, anger kindling in her belly. Why had Cassian and the others allowed this? Many of them had sons. Did they think such a fight was fair?

However, the laird had returned—and his word was law here.

And as she watched, Robert leaped forward, striking hard.

Robbie's sword flew from his hands. He staggered, slipped, and sprawled on his back in the snow.

Breathing hard, his father approached him, standing over the lad.

Robbie glared up at him.

"Ye need a lot of work on yer parrying, lad," the laird informed him. "I could have gutted ye thrice, if I'd wanted."

Elizabeth had heard enough.

Picking up her skirts, she trudged across the snow, her belly churning with rage. "He's half yer size, Robert."

The laird tore his gaze from his son's face, surprise flickering in his brown eyes. He clearly was taken aback to see her out here.

"Elizabeth." His use of her full name was a warning. "A man's size doesn't matter ... clumsy blade-work does."

"He's only ten winters old," she countered, stopping a few yards back as Robbie rolled to his feet.

"Ma," her son began, his face flushing. "All is well ... he's right, I'm—"

She cut him off, her gaze spearing her husband's. "No, he's a bully."

Silence fell in the lower ward bailey then. Snow swirled like apple blossom caught in a wind gust. The flakes settled on Robert's hair and short beard. His son forgotten, he moved toward her, and as he closed in,

Elizabeth noted that snowflakes now frosted his eyelashes.

Robert had always had lovely long eyelashes—lashes his son had inherited.

However, the gaze behind them had gone hard.

She'd succeeded in angering him.

Good. Anger was easier to weather than the cold detachment she'd witnessed in his eyes till now.

Wordlessly, Robert caught her by the arm and steered her toward the armory. "We need to have a word," he said, each word clipped. "*Without* an audience."

V

DREDGING UP THE PAST

ELIZABETH LET HIM lead her into the armory. Quite a crowd had gathered to watch father and son spar, and, like Robert, she didn't wish to give them a spectacle.

Even if fury now pulsed like a stoked ember in her gut.

Twin cressets burned on the walls of the armory—a long building that smelled of iron. Spears and blades hung from the walls, but Robert paid the weapons no mind.

Instead, he turned to Elizabeth the moment the door closed behind them, his face pale, his jaw rigid. "What kind of mother undermines her son like that?"

Elizabeth drew herself up. "And what kind of father humiliates his young son like that? The devil take ye, Rob … ye've only been back less than a day. Is a ten-year-old lad such a threat to ye that ye couldn't wait to assert yer dominance over him?"

Robert sucked in a sharp breath, as if she had landed a physical blow. "That wasn't what I was doing," he replied through gritted teeth. "God's bones, woman … the lad barely knows how to hold a sword. Instead, ye have let him become a smith's apprentice."

"Connell's been kind to him," she growled back. "And the work has done him good."

Robert's lip curled. "Aye, that's what Robbie told me too … looks like ye have him firmly clinging to yer skirts."

"Well, his father hasn't been here to guide him."

The moment the words were out, Elizabeth regretted them.

Her husband's face hardened—the light of the cressets highlighted the lean, angular lines of his cheekbones.

"No, he hasn't," Robert said when the brittle silence between them drew out. "I was availing myself of fine English hospitality ... enjoying my daily weevil-infested bread and gristle stew."

Elizabeth heaved in a deep breath. "This would never have happened ... if ye hadn't ridden out to the English that day," she said. The sharpness of her tone made her inwardly wince. *I sound like a fish-wife.* But this time she didn't regret her words.

Robert's expression changed, his gaze narrowing.

There it was—the thing that had been building between them ever since her husband's return the day before.

She knew he remembered their last words—how she'd begged him not to ride out on that last campaign. Misgiving had dogged her steps for days before he left. She'd slept fitfully and had been visited by dark dreams.

But when she'd shared her fears with Robert, he'd dismissed them.

They'd argued, and then he'd left the next day. A month later, word arrived at Dunnottar that Robert had been captured by the English in a skirmish near the River Cree, on the south-west border.

And when the news arrived, part of her hadn't been surprised.

Elizabeth had sensed in her bones that Robert's last campaign was ill-fated, but he'd been too bull-headed to heed her.

The silence drew out for a few heartbeats, and then Robert moved toward her, closing the space between them. His presence dominated the armory, and despite that she wasn't afraid of him, Elizabeth backed up.

Three steps brought her hard up against the armory door.

Robert shifted close and placed a hand on the door near her head, leaning in so that their faces were only inches apart. "I've never forgotten, Liz," he said, his voice roughening. "The last words between us were angry ones."

Elizabeth swallowed. His closeness was getting too much. Despite that the snow fell outside, it suddenly felt hot and airless inside the armory.

Part of her didn't want to dredge up the past—didn't want to go over the things they'd said to each other on that last morning.

But it hung over them like a brooding storm cloud.

His mouth quirked, his gaze holding hers. "What ... aren't ye going to tell me how right ye were? Now's yer chance."

Elizabeth wet her lips. "I didn't want to be right, Rob," she replied, her voice barely above a whisper. "I prayed I was mistaken."

"But ye weren't," he whispered back.

They stared at each other for a long moment—the tension between them rising further.

Elizabeth's pulse quickened. She didn't want to fight with him, didn't want his return home to be laced with bitterness. But she couldn't help what she felt—and nor would she stand by while he took his ill-mood out on their son.

"Ye could have heeded me," she said eventually, but yer pride wouldn't let ye."

"And ye could have just let me make my own choices."

"But yer choices don't just affect ye, do they?" she shot back, ire erupting within her once more. "Ye left us alone ... left yer brother to rule. Left me imagining the worst." She broke off there, breathing hard as she tried to stem the tide of words that surged up within her.

Eight years of words.

"Why didn't ye tell me of the siege upon Dunnottar?" he grated out the question. "Surely, as laird, I shouldn't have to wait for my steward to tell me such things."

"I was going to," Elizabeth replied, her belly clenching. "But last night … ye seemed so weary. I didn't want to burden ye."

"Burden me?" He stared down at her, a nerve flickering under his right eye, betraying the stress he was under. "I'm yer husband, not yer son. I don't need to be protected."

Elizabeth drew in a sharp breath, heat flushing through her. How dare he?

Robert glared down at her, their gazes locked in silent combat. The rasp of their breathing filled the armory.

And then, unexpectedly, he lowered his head and kissed her.

The embrace was bruising, desperate. Robert's lips crushed against hers, before his tongue sought entrance. And despite her fury, her frustration, Elizabeth welcomed him.

She drank him in like the first gulp of cool ale at the end of a hot summer's day. She'd forgotten how good he tasted, how his kisses had always been able to scatter her wits to the four winds.

His mouth never leaving hers, he stepped closer still, his long, lean body crushing hers against the door.

Elizabeth gasped at the feel of him; it brought her alive after so long, made her yearn for something she'd forgotten.

The sweet oblivion of being kissed by Robert De Keith.

Her hands went to his chest, her fingers curling against his leather vest. His kiss was wild, dominant— how she loved it.

Words had failed them both, and so now he was trying to bridge the gulf between them with his body.

It would be easy to give in to it, to the sensual promise of his questing tongue, to the rasp of his short beard against her cheek.

But even if he lifted her skirts and took her against the door, even if she let him lose himself in her, it wouldn't change the fact that the man who'd returned to her wasn't the man she remembered.

Elizabeth's fingers tightened into fists against his chest, and—mustering all her will—she ripped her mouth from his, turning her face to the side as she sucked in a deep, steadying breath.

Her treacherous body sang for him.

They'd wounded each other—had both drawn blood with barbed words. Giving into this wouldn't change anything.

"Liz." His voice was a rasp, a plea. "What's wrong?"

Tears stung her eyelids as she closed her eyes.

Everything.

"Ye have been away too long," she replied, cursing the tremble in her own voice. "I don't know ye anymore."

"Some things ye haven't forgotten," he replied huskily. "Yer body remembers ... even if *ye* don't."

Her head snapped around, and she met his gaze once more.

Curse him, she wished he wouldn't look at her like that—the man had a stare that could melt stone.

Her body was weak—but fortunately her wits had returned to her. Robert was her husband, but they were indeed strangers. She hadn't liked the man who'd just humiliated his ten-year-old son, the man who couldn't even hold a conversation with her, who was openly suspicious of her.

There had always been a strong attraction between them. From the first moment they'd been introduced— the young, headstrong laird of Dunnottar and laird Strachan's eldest daughter. It had been a union to bind two clans, but right from the beginning, just a look from Robert had set her blood aflame.

It should have come as no surprise that even after so many years apart, the heat was still there.

VI

AWAY TOO LONG

ROBERT WATCHED HIS wife leave the armory. A stone had settled upon his chest, yet he made no move to stop her.

The look on her face when she'd pulled away had struck him like a blow.

The reserve in her eyes, especially after such a heated kiss, made it difficult to draw breath.

And yet he said nothing.

He just let her go.

The armory door thudded shut, leaving Robert alone.

He moved back, leaning against a high wooden bench where rows of helmets were neatly stacked.

Ye have been away too long ... I don't know ye anymore.

Elizabeth's words repeated themselves over and over in his head.

Robert clenched his jaw.

That made two of them.

Did she think he liked being this way? All those years in that tiny, damp cell had eroded away at him. He'd spent too long alone with his own thoughts—and in the end, they'd turned on him.

Robert lifted a hand to his lips, where the sting of their fierce kiss still remained.

Just for a few instants, he'd forgotten himself.

They'd both been angry, had both sought to wound the other—but the moment he'd kissed her, none of it had mattered.

She'd tasted as sweet as heather honey, her soft curves pressed against him, her mouth as eager as his.

But although her body was willing, her soul wasn't.

Robert wasn't the only one who'd changed. The Elizabeth he remembered always had a ready smile and a laugh that brought sunlight into even the dullest day.

Yet smiles didn't come easily to his wife now. There was a severity to her that had been absent last time he'd seen her.

Of course, she'd been laird for years now—a responsibility indeed. And she'd believed herself a widow. She could have taken another husband, although with his death unconfirmed, the church would take a dim view.

Such things happened nonetheless.

And yet, Elizabeth had remained faithful to his memory.

Robert muttered a curse and dragged a hand down his face.

Damn it all—he was doing a poor job of reuniting with his family.

"The accounts are all in good order … our coffers are healthy indeed." Robert glanced up from the ledger, meeting Donnan De Keith's eye.

The steward of Dunnottar smiled back. "Aye … we've had a few lean years, especially with all the problems Longshanks and his son have caused us. But yer wife has managed yer lands well … even if yer brother nearly brought us to ruin."

At the mention of his younger brother, David, Robert scowled. Laird and steward sat at a table in the center of the solar, enjoying cups of warmed mead while they went over the accounts together. Robert had been back at Dunnottar two days now, and was happy to resume his duties as laird. Donnan had just been filling him in on some of the other events that had taken place over the past eight years.

"So, Shaw Irvine turned against us," Robert murmured when the steward had concluded his summary. "The bastard broke our truce."

Donnan nodded, his own brow furrowing. "Aye … we were all shocked when he joined with Longshanks as he lay siege to Dunnottar."

"And how did Gavina take the news of her brother's treachery?"

Lady Gavina Irvine had been wed to his brother—a match Robert had been instrumental in organizing. It was a marriage that David had resented him for, for he'd never wanted to wed an Irvine, even if the Irvine laird's daughter was a beauty. Later, Gavina's brother had broken the peace between the two clans and even sided with the English during the siege of Dunnottar.

Now heavily pregnant with her third child to her current husband, Gavina still resided in Dunnottar. Her man, a warrior named Draco, worked in the Dunnottar Guard. Robert had caught a glimpse of Gavina earlier as he re-entered the keep; the contentment on the woman's face these days was a stark contrast to how pale and strained she'd once been.

After David's death, Gavina had forfeited her position as laird by wedding Draco—but she hardly seemed to care.

"She was as upset as the rest of us," Donnan replied. "And she didn't shed a tear when news of Irvine's death reached us."

Robert leaned back in his chair and took a sip of mead. "How did the bastard die?"

The steward's mouth curved into a humorless smile. He'd aged a lot since Robert had seen him last, his once brown hair almost entirely grey. However, his gaze was as sharp as ever. "They say it was a hunting accident."

Robert cocked an eyebrow, encouraging the steward to continue.

Donnan cast him a sly look. "It was well known that the Wallace wanted his guts. After William left Dunnottar … I'd wager he paid Irvine a wee visit at Drum Castle."

Robert took this news in before he smiled. "We have much to thank the Wallace for, it seems."

Indeed, the Wallace had come to their aid years earlier—when the English had taken the stronghold. He'd burned the English garrison to death in the chapel—and the walls of it still bore char marks. However, when he'd eventually chosen Dunnottar as his hiding place, he'd brought Edward of England's wrath down upon them all.

Robert's smile faded. They were both dead now— William Wallace and 'The Hammer of the Scots'—but the turmoil that had plagued this land for years now hadn't died with them. Edward's son was proving to be as problematic as his father had been.

Loosing a deep breath, Robert met the steward's eye once more. "God's teeth, Donnan … why do I suddenly feel weary of it all?" He pulled a face. "I think I'm getting old."

Donnan snorted. "Ye are still a pup compared to an old hound like me." His gaze searched Robert's face. "Ye have just suffered a lot … and it will take time for ye to feel yer old self again."

Robert looked away, at where the hearth crackled and popped, casting a warm embrace over them both.

Maybe Donnan was right. He expected much of himself, and of Elizabeth. He needed to leave his past resentments and hurts behind—or he would never find the peace that currently eluded him.

Elizabeth deserved better than the bitter husk that had returned to her.

"Are ye not happy to have Rob home?"

Gavina's question hit Elizabeth in the breast like a well-aimed quarrel. She paused her work on the holly-wreath she was fashioning and glanced up. "Of course I am."

Even to her, the words seemed forced.

And of course, Gavina wasn't fooled. "Ye don't look pleased," she observed, reaching for a length of red ribbon to tie on the wreath she was making.

The two women sat near the hearth in the women's solar—hard at work on Yuletide decorations. The 'Long Night' was swiftly approaching.

There were still many preparations to be made, and Elizabeth was glad of it, for the tasks took her mind off her churning belly and her memory of that searing kiss she'd shared with Robert the day before. She'd avoided him ever since, but the time was coming when they'd have to speak again.

She was dreading it.

Elizabeth heaved in a deep breath. "I've never been able to hide much from ye, have I?"

Gavina's mouth curved. "Nor I ye ... that's why we are as close as sisters."

Their gazes met, and warmth seeped through Elizabeth. She had two younger sisters, but she hadn't seen either in years, and they'd never been close as bairns. Gavina didn't have any sisters—and had only been cursed with a treacherous elder brother. During Gavina's first years at Dunnottar, the women's relationship had been pleasant but interlaced by formality—they'd been sisters-by-marriage rather than friends. But the years had forged a bond between them, and once Gavina wed Draco, it was impossible not to be drawn to the happiness that emanated from her.

The door to the women's solar opened then, and two pretty brown-haired women hurried in. One had smoke-grey eyes and a slender build, while the other possessed grey-green eyes and lush curves.

Aila Gaius and Heather Cato—the steward's daughters. These days, Aila was wed to the Captain of the Dunnottar Guard, while Heather now lived with her husband and two daughters in nearby Stonehaven.

The sisters carried large baskets filled with ivy, mistletoe, pine sprigs, and holly. Their faces were flushed with cold as they hurried toward Elizabeth and Gavina.

"Sorry, we're late," Aila gasped. "Callum had a tumble in the snow this morning … it took me a while to calm him."

Gavina frowned at this news. "Did he hurt himself?"

Aila shook her head. "Just a fat lip and bruised pride. His brother won't stop tormenting him over it."

Despite her low mood, Elizabeth found herself smiling. Callum and Duncan, born just eighteen months apart, were both tempests, despite that they were only aged four and six.

"It took me an age to get here from Stonehaven this morning," Heather announced, taking her place at the table. She then started to pull out the various items she'd collected for wreath-making. "The snow's deep for this time of year … it was up to my knees in places."

"Here." Elizabeth passed Heather a cup of warmed mead. "This should make the blood return to yer toes."

Heather grinned back at her, before she wrapped her pale fingers around the cup, lifting it to her lips.

Elizabeth watched her, her mood lifting just a little. Heather and Aila were such vibrant company, although now that Heather had moved out of the castle, they didn't see as much of her as previously.

Aila set down her basket on the table and took a seat. Her gaze flicked from Gavina to Elizabeth, where it rested. "How is Robert settling back in?"

Elizabeth tensed. She'd been relieved to have her conversation with Gavina interrupted—she really didn't want to answer questions about Robert at present.

Sensing Elizabeth's mood, Aila's expression clouded. "What's wrong?"

"Nothing," Elizabeth lied. Heather was now watching her, a groove etched between her brows. "It's just taking a bit of getting used to ... having my husband home again."

"It must feel ... strange," Aila agreed. Her expression turned speculative then, and Elizabeth realized that Cassian had likely told her about the incident in the lower ward bailey.

"It does," Elizabeth replied, heaviness settling upon her. "We aren't the same people we once were ... and we're both struggling to come to terms with that."

VII

DECORATING THE HALL

ELIZABETH KNOCKED GENTLY on the door. "Come in," Father Finlay's voice greeted her. She pushed the door open to find two figures bent over an open book seated near a glowing hearth. Robbie was haltingly reading out verb conjugations in French, while the chaplain patiently corrected him.

Robbie glanced up. Usually, if Elizabeth interrupted his lessons with the chaplain, her son favored her with a beaming smile. The lad found hours of Latin and French drills tedious and was always looking for an escape.

This afternoon though, his gaze was wary.

Elizabeth had seen little of him since the incident in the lower ward bailey the day before.

If she hadn't known better, she'd think her son was avoiding her.

"I need yer help in the hall," she greeted her son with a smile before shifting her attention to Father Finlay. "Can I steal Robbie away a little early, Father?"

Did she imagine it, or did relief flare in the chaplain's dark eyes? Robbie was a challenging student at the best of times—and since his father's return to Dunnottar, the lad was understandably distracted. "As luck would have it, we were about to conclude our lessons for the day, My Lady." Father Finlay deftly closed the book Robbie had been reciting from. "Off ye go, lad."

Robbie nodded and rose to his feet. However, he hardly looked joyful at being let away early. Wordlessly, he followed his mother from the chamber.

Elizabeth led the way down the stairs to the long gallery below that would take them to Dunnottar's hall. Finally, when the silence between them drew out, she cut him a glance. "Are ye angry with me, Robbie?"

"No, Ma," he replied quickly—too quickly.

"Ye wish I hadn't interceded yesterday?"

A silence followed, and it was only when the oaken doors to the hall loomed ahead that her son answered. "Ye made a fuss about nothing, Ma ... we were only sparring."

Elizabeth's spine stiffened. Was that what everyone looking on thought too—that she was an overbearing wife and over-protective mother?

"He's three times yer size, Robbie," she replied, trying to keep the hurt out of her voice. "Ye are too young to spar with a blade."

"But it's made of wood," the lad burst out. "And father ... Da ... says that he learned how to wield a sword when he was younger than me."

Elizabeth's jaw tightened. Why didn't that comment surprise her? Robert had been brought up to be a warrior—and he wanted his son to follow him. They were all warriors, the De Keith men.

Pushing open the doors to the hall, Elizabeth led the way inside. Earlier in the day, the hall had been a flurry of activity as servants decorated the long tables with wreaths of holly and pine. The resinous scent of pine now filled the air, blending with the pungent smell of peat-smoke drifting from the fire.

Not replying to Robbie's earlier comment, Elizabeth motioned to the ladder leaning against one wall. "I need someone young and agile to hang mistletoe and ivy from the rafters."

Her son nodded, his expression now earnest.

Elizabeth's chest constricted.

Robbie was a good lad—and he always tried so hard to please her. Robert, curse him, was right when he'd accused her of cossetting the lad.

He was all she had. For years now, it had been her and Robbie against the world.

The thought of any harm befalling him made her break out in a cold sweat.

Forcing down her anxiety, Elizabeth passed her son a basket of mistletoe and flashed him a smile. "Up ye go then ... I'll hold the ladder."

Heavy oaken beams, blackened with smoke from the fire, hung overhead.

Elizabeth held the ladder tight while Robbie scaled it, racing up like a squirrel.

"There are hooks up there," she called to him. "Just hook the mistletoe over them."

Her son did as bid, finishing the task in moments. He then slid down the ladder, a grin plastered on his face.

Why was it that lads loved to climb and teeter from great heights? At the same age, Elizabeth had been content to play with her poppets and embroider pillowcases. It seemed that from the moment they could walk, lads went looking for danger. Elizabeth wanted to protect him from it, but she knew the day was swiftly coming when she couldn't.

They shifted the ladder to the next beam, and Robbie scaled the ladder once more—this time with a basket of ivy.

He'd just started to hang it when the doors to the hall opened and a tall man strode inside.

Elizabeth's grip on the ladder tightened at the sight of her husband walking toward her.

Curse him, but Robert drew her eye as much as he ever had. Dressed in leather braies and a velvet lèine, a snowy ermine stole around his shoulders with his brown hair spilling over it, he looked every inch the laird.

"Da!" Robbie called out.

Something twisted in Elizabeth's chest. The eagerness in Robbie's voice caused a strange jealousy to rise inside her. All these years taking care of her son, raising him, and his father only had to walk back into his life to alter their relationship forever.

Robbie had appeared cowed after being trounced by his father in the lower ward bailey—Elizabeth had expected the incident would make him wary around his father, but it seemed that wasn't the case.

"Making yerself useful I see," Robert greeted his son. "Good lad."

"Aye … Ma doesn't want to climb the ladder," Robbie replied. "So I'm hanging the decorations instead."

Robert smiled—and Elizabeth caught her breath. It was the first real smile she'd seen since his return.

A pity then that it wasn't for her.

"Just one more beam should do it," Elizabeth told Robbie. Her voice had a brittle note to it—but she couldn't help herself.

She'd been enjoying having her son's full attention. But the moment his father walked into the hall, she was all but forgotten.

"Aye, Ma … shall I hang up some fir boughs on this one?"

"Go on then."

Robert stopped a few yards away, watching silently as Robbie finished his task.

When the lad slid back down to the floor, empty basket in hand, Robert glanced around, taking in his surroundings. "I'd forgotten how grand this hall is," he murmured. His gaze went to the De Keith banner hanging over the hearth and the motto inscribed there: *Veritas Vincit*—Truth prevails.

Elizabeth saw his gaze rest there, and noted how his handsome features tensed.

Did truth always conquer all? Elizabeth had been brutally honest with him in the armory—but it hadn't cleared the air between them. Instead, it had created a gulf.

"I like the smell of Yuletide, Robbie announced. "It's like standing in a pine-thicket."

Robert tore his gaze from the banner. "Aye, lad … do ye fancy a ride out tomorrow if the weather clears a little? We can see if we can flush out some deer in the woods north of here."

Robbie's face lit up like a candle. "Aye, Da!"

Robert approached the lad then, and to Elizabeth's surprise, he reached out and ruffled Robbie's hair. It was the first gesture of affection toward his son she'd seen since his return. Perhaps their altercation the day before had made him think on things?

Even so, Robert's suggestion made Elizabeth tense. Heather had said the snow was deep; she didn't want Robbie to hurt himself.

"Run along now, lad," Robert continued with another smile. "I wish to have a word with yer Ma."

"Can we all have supper together today?" Robbie asked, the hope in his voice almost painful. The lad had clearly gotten over his bashfulness in regard to his father.

Being knocked flat on his back by the man had shattered Robbie's reserve.

Elizabeth's mouth thinned. Sometimes she didn't understand males at all.

"Aye ... that sounds like a fine idea," Robert replied, still smiling. "Ye can join us in my solar."

With a hurried 'goodbye' to Elizabeth, Robbie rushed off, the hall doors thudding shut behind him.

Silence followed as Robert's gaze settled upon her.

"Ye have clearly impressed someone," she said, inwardly cringing at the bitter edge to her voice.

Robert's mouth curved. "Aye ... but not ye it seems."

He approached her then.

Elizabeth stood her ground, although the memory of what had passed between them last time he'd moved close, of the passionate kiss they'd shared, made her pulse quicken.

"The snow's too deep to take a bairn out riding," she said after a pause.

Robert made an irritated sound at the back of his throat. "God's teeth, woman, the lad longs for some adventure." His gaze fused with hers. "Sooner or later, ye are going to have to let him grow up."

Elizabeth sucked in a deep breath. "He's still a bairn, Rob. Don't wish these years away ... once they're gone, they're gone forever."

He snorted. "Taking the lad out on a ride isn't going to catapult him into manhood." He moved in closer still, towering over her now. And when he spoke again, his tone had softened. "I'll not take him from ye, Liz. A son needs a father, that's all."

Elizabeth held his gaze, her throat thickening. Damn him, but the man had read her too well. He'd always done so in the past, yet the detached stranger who'd returned to her had appeared incapable of such empathy.

But as she stared into his eyes, Elizabeth wondered if some of the man she'd once loved still remained.

VIII

STARTING AFRESH

"CAN YE PASS me the bread, Robbie?" Elizabeth's request broke the tense silence in the laird's solar.

The three of them sat at the huge polished table—a light supper of braised cabbage, goat's cheese, and fresh oaten bread before them. In the days leading up to Yule, the folk of Dunnottar avoided meat and ate simply, in preparation for the feasting that was to follow.

The roaring hearth cut through a cold evening. Outdoors the snow had ceased for a while, although a biting wind had sprung up, whistling in from the frozen north. It rattled the shutters and pushed its way in through any gaps it could find, causing a draft that made the flames in the hearth dance.

Robbie did as bid, his gaze shifting to his father though. "Captain Gaius chose a pony for me last summer ... he's a garron named 'Hunter'."

At the far end of the table, the laird smiled before lifting his pewter goblet to his lips. "A fine name for a pony."

"He's hardy," Robbie assured his father. "A wee bit of snow won't bother Hunter."

"Even so ... if there's a blizzard, ye won't be riding out in it." Elizabeth spoke up, only to earn a reproachful look from her son. She didn't like the role she'd unconsciously stepped into since her husband's reappearance—that of watchdog. However, the words of censure flew from her mouth before she could prevent herself.

With a jolt, she realized that part of her sought to undermine Robert.

She'd been in charge here until two days ago, and although the responsibilities of laird had weighed upon her at times, she realized now that the power was hard to give up. She was supposed to revert to the role she'd had before Robert's capture—that of biddable wife.

Women's work was her ken now, the bigger decisions were not.

"This is a good supper," Robert offered when silence stretched out once more. "Ye have no idea how I missed Scottish fare."

"Was English food vile, Da?" Robbie asked, his gaze widening.

Robert pulled a face. "The food they served me was, at least."

"We're having spit-roasted venison for the Yuletide banquet," Robbie replied, "followed by honey cakes and clotted cream."

Robert rolled his eyes, flashing his son a grin. "Then I shall have to be careful not to gorge myself." His gaze flicked to Elizabeth then. "I have happy memories of Yule, Robbie ... yer mother and I were wed just before it."

Robbie swallowed a large mouthful. "Really?"

"Aye ... yer Ma had mistletoe in her hair, I remember ... and wore a pale blue gown. She was beautiful. She still is."

Robbie paused eating, his attention shifting to Elizabeth. "Ye are blushing Ma," he observed with a cheeky smile.

"It's warm in here." Elizabeth muttered, reaching for her own goblet of wine.

They all knew she was lying though—the heat in her cheeks had more to do with her husband's honeyed words.

I can't believe I'm so easily flattered.

Elizabeth focused on her supper then, aware that Robert was watching her. Truthfully, it had been years since she'd felt beautiful.

She'd worn widow's black for a long while after Robert's capture. After that, she'd focused on running

Dunnottar. Her busy life had left her little time for herself. As laird, she'd held a position of respect.

Men didn't flirt with her anymore.

Not until tonight.

They finished their meal—with Robbie's lively chatter providing a bridge between them. Elizabeth had never seen the lad so animated. However, when he went off to bed once supper had concluded, his parents were left alone.

Servants came and went, collecting the empty dishes and replenishing the bramble wine. Seated by the fire in high-backed wooden chairs, facing each other, Robert and Elizabeth lapsed into a drawn-out silence.

"I wasn't merely flattering ye earlier," Robert spoke up eventually. "It's the truth. I'd forgotten just how bonny ye are, Liz."

Elizabeth glanced up, her fingers tightening around the stem of her goblet. "I'm no longer the lass ye wed," she said softly. Sadness enveloped her then. "The years have taken too much from me."

"They've also given ye something." He replied, his tone firming. "Yer beauty shines stronger than I remember."

Elizabeth's breathing hitched. Part of her wished he wouldn't say such things—but another part of her craved to hear the words.

The urge to deny his compliment rose within her, but she shoved it down.

She wouldn't let bitterness ruin this moment.

"I missed ye so much," she finally whispered. "For a while, I hoped … and then after David tried to kill Longshanks that flame died within me." She lifted her goblet to her lips and took a gulp of spicy wine. "I've been harsh since ye returned, and I'm sorry for it … it's just seeing ye alive, after I'd long told myself ye were dead, is taking some time to get used to."

He huffed a laugh, his gaze meeting hers. "It's a shock to me as well … being back here again after so long. I feel like an imposter."

Elizabeth shook her head. "This is where ye belong, Rob ... even if the sweet woman ye remember has turned into a blade-tongued harpy."

He laughed, and the warm sound rolled over her, making the tension in Elizabeth's shoulders ease just a little. "Ye were never biddable, Liz ... and just as well, for I never wanted a wife who had nothing to say for herself."

He set his wine aside and rose to his feet, crossing to her.

Elizabeth stopped breathing as he gently took her wine and placed it on the mantelpiece. He then took hold of her hands and drew her to her feet.

"Ye have done well as laird," he murmured. "Donnan showed me the books ... they are healthier than I remember."

Her mouth quirked. "Is that surprise I hear in yer voice, Rob? Ye didn't believe a woman could manage this castle and its lands?"

He huffed another laugh. "If I did, I stand corrected now." He paused then, gazing down at her. "I don't want to fight ye," he murmured. "I've come home ... but I won't truly belong here until ye and I are no longer strangers."

Elizabeth let out the shaky breath she'd been holding. "Why do I feel like a nervous bride?" she whispered.

His mouth curved. "Because we're starting afresh ye and I."

He reached out, his thumb brushing her lower lip.

A soft sigh gusted out of Elizabeth. Even after all these years, his touch still had a visceral effect on her. The feel of his skin on hers made it difficult to think, let alone respond to him.

"Will ye lie with me tonight, Liz?" he finally asked. "Can we put the angry words of the past two days behind us and start again?"

"Aye," she breathed. His nearness, the heat of his body, enveloped her like a warming winter mantle. Before she even realized what she was doing, Elizabeth swayed toward him.

Robert's mouth slanted across hers then, his arms clasping about her.

Elizabeth melted into him. Her lips parted, and she hungrily welcomed his tongue. An instant later, her arms went up and entwined about his neck.

The kiss deepened, their bodies flush now.

A fevered heat rushed through Elizabeth, unleashing wildness.

Lord, it's been so long.

She'd forgotten how good he tasted, how strong and masculine his body felt pressed against her.

She clutched at his shoulders, clinging to him now as the kiss grew deeper, hotter. She wanted to crawl inside him, to forget all those long years of grief and loneliness.

An instant later, Robert pulled back from her, swept Elizabeth up in his arms, and made for the door that led into his bed-chamber. Heart thundering in her ears, Elizabeth sank against the wall of his chest, need pulsing through her now.

The laird's bed-chamber was a large, starkly-masculine space—a room that Elizabeth rarely ventured into, especially since Robert's departure.

However, it seemed fitting that he'd take her in here. In many ways, she did feel like a new bride. She suddenly ached for Robert to make her his, to let herself go completely.

He set her down on the deerskin rug before the fire, his mouth claiming hers once more.

They devoured each other now, their hands ripping at each other's clothing. Elizabeth was desperate to rid him of the layers of linen, wool, and leather that separated them.

A chill draft from the shuttered window feathered down her naked back when he stripped her lèine from her, but Elizabeth barely noticed—her attention was upon her husband's hard-muscled body.

Even though he was leaner than she remembered, he exuded a virility, a masculinity that made her lower belly catch aflame. And the sight of his shaft, rigid and swollen, made her heart leap against her ribs.

She wanted him buried deep inside her.

They sank down onto the deerskin rug then, their mouths fused, not even bothering to move to the bed. The softness of the deerskin brushed against Elizabeth's sensitized skin as she reached for Robert, pulling his naked body flush against hers.

A cry of joy escaped her when he parted her thighs and thrust into her, seating himself fully.

How she'd missed this, how she ached for him.

IX

COMING HOME

ROBERT WAS LOST. The feel of being buried deep inside his wife nearly sent him over the edge.

He was being consumed, driven to madness with wanting.

His mouth branded hers before tracing a path down her jaw and throat. She tasted so sweet, and the softness of her lush body under his felt as if he held heaven in his hands.

For so many years, he'd dreamed of this, longed for this—and then finally, in the last years of his imprisonment, he'd thought he'd never again lie with his wife.

He'd lost hope.

But here they were.

Robert withdrew from her—something that required a great act of will—and moved down, grasping her breasts and pushing them up into his face. He suckled them hard, feasting on their fullness while Elizabeth writhed beneath him.

She was making soft mewling noises, her eyes closed, and a look of intense rapture on her face.

It was too much—he had to be inside her again. Now.

Robert plunged into Elizabeth, holding himself up above his wife as he took her in deep, hard strokes. She cried out, arching up to meet each thrust. Reaching up, she clutched at his shoulders, her fingernails digging into his skin.

He continued to thrust into her, the wet sounds of their coupling filling the chamber. When Robert's climax finally slammed into him, it caught him with such force that his vision dimmed for an instant. He was vaguely aware of Elizabeth's cries, the shudders that wracked her body—as he arched back, a ragged shout tearing from his throat.

Breathing hard, he collapsed, before propping himself up on his elbows, lest he crushed her. Likewise, Elizabeth panted, sweat gleaming upon her naked skin, illuminated by the fire's warm glow.

Their gazes met and held—a long, silent moment passing between them.

A moment that Robert was loath to fill with words.

Elizabeth reached up, her fingertips tracing the line of her husband's face.

In the firelight, he looked younger, more vulnerable.

It was the face of the man she'd fallen in love with fifteen years earlier.

The man she thought she'd lost forever.

He was still buried inside her, and she never wanted him to leave—never wanted this feeling of completeness to end. She'd thought their first time together after so many years would be awkward: two strangers pretending they were still a couple, despite the gulf between them.

Yet the evening had brought clarity.

Perhaps the conflict between them had been necessary after all, for it had eventually led them here.

"Am I still a stranger to ye?" Robert eventually asked, his smile tentative, boyish even.

Elizabeth smiled back, her fingers trailing down to his chest, where she traced the whorls of crisp hair. "Perhaps not," she murmured, suddenly feeling as shy as a maid at her first dance.

"We fit together even better than I remember," he continued, his voice lowering to a sultry rumble.

"Aye, we do," she whispered.

He reached out then, his fingers tangling in her thick dark-blonde hair, which was spread out on the deerskin. "Ye always brought out the best in me," he continued, his throat bobbing. "I fear that without ye ... I'd let bitterness and anger consume me."

She heaved in a deep breath. "I'm not surprised." Elizabeth paused there, searching his face. "Were they cruel to ye?"

Their gazes fused, and then his mouth quirked. "I was given a good beating when I arrived at Warkworth, and another when I kicked one of the guards in the cods ... but after I learned my place, my English captors left me alone." He broke off there, his face turning somber. "The loneliness was the worst," he said finally. "It wears down on ye ... makes yer mind turn against ye." He paused there, his gaze shadowing. "And when I never heard from ye, my imagination ran away with me."

"Ye know Edward refused to tell me where ye were imprisoned?" Elizabeth asked, her fingers clasping around his. "I was convinced that Longshanks would kill ye in retribution for what David did."

The words hung between them, a reminder of how fortunate Robert was not to have been hanged.

A moment later, Robert's mouth curved. "Lucky for me, Longshanks had more pressing issues to attend to at the time."

His gaze turned limpid then, and he raised Elizabeth's hand to his lips, kissing the back of it softly. "Life has given me a second chance, Liz ... and I don't intend to waste it."

Heat spread across Elizabeth's chest at these words, at the huskiness in his voice.

She gasped then, as she felt him stiffen inside her—and a delicious ache started to pulse in her lower belly. She wanted him again, wanted to chase away all the dark memories, all the loneliness that had plagued them both.

She lifted her hips to him, undulating them in a slow and sensual roll that dragged a deep groan from her husband.

Then Robert's mouth crushed down on hers, and all rational thought fled.

"It's a fine day for a ride," Cassian Gaius announced, squinting up at the hard blue sky … just keep away from the cliffs."

Robert snorted at the warning. He'd grown up at Dunnottar, and knew just how perilous some areas could be when covered in snow. "We'll ride to the oakwood, west of Stonehaven," he replied, swinging up onto the saddle. This morning he sat astride a bay courser, while Robbie perched atop Hunter, his shaggy garron.

The Highland pony tossed its head, eager to be off. After days being cooped up, Hunter longed to stretch his legs.

Robert met his son's gaze. "Ready, lad?"

Robbie nodded, excitement glinting in his eyes.

Reining his horse around, Robert urged it toward the gates. "We'll be back mid-afternoon at the latest," he called over his shoulder. "In time for the first ladles of mulled wine."

Tonight was the eve of Yule. Night would fall early, and then the residents of the keep would gather in the hall to set fire to the great oaken log in the hearth, drink mulled wine, and feast on the first of the Yuletide treats: game pie followed by aged cheeses. Haunches of roast venison would be served the following day.

Leaving the walls of Dunnottar behind, Robert let his courser pick its way down the snowy defile and up the steep bank to the cliff-top opposite.

It hadn't snowed for a few hours now, and the snow lay in a pristine white crust for miles around. With the winter sun sparkling off it, the whiteness was blinding.

Reaching the cliff-top, Robert drew in a deep breath of sharp, cold air.

A smile then spread across his face.

For the first time in days, he truly felt like he'd come home.

Last night would forever remain etched in his memory.

Liz, her creamy limbs spread open to receive him, her blue eyes dark with passion, and her cries filling the bed-chamber.

And when they hadn't been making love, they'd talked—long into the night.

With the rising of the sun, Robert De Keith felt as if he were twenty once more. He'd told Elizabeth that, as they'd curled up together, exhausted in bed—and her mouth had curved. "Ye certainly have the lustiness of a young man," she'd murmured.

He'd favored her with a cheeky grin. "It's incredible what having a beautiful woman in yer bed can do for a man."

Robert's body still felt relaxed in the aftermath of that torrid night, his limbs loose. He looked forward to taking Elizabeth to his bed again tonight and exploring her delicious body once again.

However, for now it was a brisk, bright morning, and he'd promised his son a ride.

They rode out across the snow-covered hills, and Robert noticed that his son's mount was indeed in high spirits. The garron side-stepped and danced, as it snorted and tossed its head. As Robert looked on, the pony bucked, nearly dislodging its rider.

"Hunter's a feisty one," Robert commented. "Unusual for a garron."

"He's often too sluggish," Robbie informed him, his face tensing. He was struggling to keep his mount in check. "So I fed him half a bucket of oats last night."

Robert frowned at this news. "Well, that'll do it," he replied. "I'd say he's got energy to burn now ... let's stretch his legs."

With that, he urged his courser into a canter, kicking up snow behind them. "Race ye to the woods!"

X

THE FADING LIGHT

"YE ARE LOOKING pleased with yerself," Gavina greeted Elizabeth with a knowing smile. "Ye look like a cat that's just caught a nice fat thrush."

Elizabeth smiled back. "The sun is shining for the first time in days." She motioned to the swath of blue sky out the open window she perched next to.

It was a bit too cold to stay by the window for long— but the fresh air chased away the lingering peat smoke.

Elizabeth was enjoying the sting of cold air on her cheeks—and she couldn't wipe the grin off her face. Happiness bathed her in warmth as if she were standing next to a roaring heath.

Last night had been unexpected.

Last night had been wonderful.

She turned her attention fully to Gavina then as she approached the window. Her friend looked tired this morning, and uncomfortable. That belly of hers was quite a weight for such a small woman to carry.

"I have my husband back," Elizabeth said softly.

Gavina's cornflower-blue eyes gleamed. "It warms my heart to hear ye say that," she replied. "Relations between ye seemed so ... strained."

"They were ... but things are different now," Elizabeth assured her.

Gavina grimaced then, a hand settling upon her swollen belly.

Elizabeth frowned. "Is something amiss?"

"No," Gavina replied with another grimace. "I just feel like an over-stuffed sack of oats these days."

Elizabeth laughed, moving away from the window. "Come." She guided Gavina over to one of the chairs flanking the hearth. "Sit down for a bit."

"I shouldn't really." Gavina muttered. "I've left the bairns with Draco ... lord knows what mischief they'll get up to."

Elizabeth cocked an eyebrow. "He's usually the one who instigates such trouble."

"Aye ... and he's got them down in the kitchens with the cooks, helping make sausages for tomorrow's banquet. I should really rescue the poor cooks."

Nonetheless, Gavina did as Elizabeth bid, lowering herself with a groan into one of the chairs.

Smiling, Elizabeth pulled up a chair opposite. "It's incredible how things turn out," she murmured. "Who'd have thought ten years ago that we'd all be where we are now?"

Gavina glanced up, her eyes crinkling at the corners when she smiled. "Aye ... Robert had yet to be captured, William Wallace was still alive, and I was wed to David." Her smile dimmed then. "I never thought I'd find such happiness, Liz. Sometimes I look at my husband and our bairns and wonder how I managed to find fortune's favor."

"Ye are more worthy of it than many," Elizabeth replied. "I must admit when ye first wed Draco, I thought it would be yer ruin ... but ye two have proven to be a great match." Elizabeth paused there. "I think ye bring out the best in each other."

Gavina smiled back. "As ye and Robert always did."

Warmth seeped through Elizabeth. Aye, it was true. They had once been a good match—and after last night, she hoped that they could again be happy together.

"It must have been difficult for the pair of ye though," Gavina said, her gaze roaming Elizabeth's face. "Eight years is a long time to be apart ... and ye have both been through much."

"He is different to the man I recall," Elizabeth admitted. "But I hope—"

She cut off there as opposite her Gavina gave a sharp gasp.

A tinkling noise followed.

Dropping her gaze to the flagstones, Elizabeth saw clear liquid pooling there.

Elizabeth rose to her feet, excitement climbing within her. "Yer waters have broken!" She stepped forward, taking her friend by the hands and helping her stand. "The bairn is coming … just in time for Yule!"

The light was starting to fade when Elizabeth emerged from Gavina's bed-chamber.

Draco was pacing up and down the hallway outside, his hawkish features taut with worry.

Glancing up, his dark gaze speared Elizabeth. "The babe. Has it come?"

"Not yet," Elizabeth replied. "Although it's on its way … her birthing pains grow strong." She gestured to the door behind her. "Keep Gavina company while I go and collect some swaddling linen and hot water."

Seeing the worry in Draco's eyes, she favored him with a reassuring smile. "All is well … I'll be back soon."

Hurrying down the hallway to the stairwell that would take her downstairs, Elizabeth wondered how her husband and son's ride had gone earlier in the day.

She passed a narrow window in the stairwell and noted that the sky was darkening rapidly, and that it had started snowing again.

She'd been so preoccupied with Gavina she'd barely noticed the passing of time.

Dunnottar didn't have a resident healer or midwife—and Elizabeth had taken up the roles. Helping a woman give birth was a great responsibility, but like her mother before her, she was a skilled healer and competent midwife.

Even so, she wouldn't be able to relax until Gavina delivered her bairn safely.

Childbirth was always such a risky time for women.

On the way down to the kitchens and laundry, Elizabeth made a detour to the laird's apartments—no doubt Robert and Robbie would be warming themselves by the fire with cups of warm wine.

However, she found the laird's solar empty—and when she went to her own quarters, they weren't there either.

Maybe they've gone to the hall already? She really had to collect the clean linen and hot water. But first, she wanted to see her husband and son, and to know how their day had gone.

In the gallery leading to the hall, she encountered the castle's steward, Donnan de Keith. He limped toward her, a grin splitting his face.

"I hear Gavina is about to give birth," he greeted her.

"Aye," Elizabeth replied with a distracted smile. "It's not far away now." She met Donnan's eye. "Have ye just come from the hall?"

"Aye."

"Are the laird and Robbie there?"

The steward shook his head. "Not yet, My Lady."

Elizabeth stilled. "Have they not returned from their ride?"

Donnan's brow furrowed. "I didn't realize they'd gone out," he answered. "Maybe they're stabling their horses now."

"I'll go and see," Elizabeth replied. A chill sense of foreboding rose within her then, a gnawing intuition that something was wrong.

Without another word to Donnan, she turned and fled toward the entrance hall.

The snow fell heavily in the lower ward bailey, thick flakes swirling and fluttering silently. The glow of torchlight and braziers illuminated the wide space.

Gathering her fur mantle close, Elizabeth hurried to the stables, her boots sinking into the snow.

Inside, she found stable lads feeding the horses their evening mash. Cassian was there too, saddling his courser.

He glanced up, his features tensing when he saw Elizabeth step inside the stables, her gaze darting around. "My Lady?"

"The laird and Robbie ... are they back yet?"

Cassian shook his head. "I expected them back a couple of hours ago ... I'm going out to look for them."

Elizabeth drew in a sharp breath.

"They can't have gone far," Cassian replied hurriedly, seeing her look of alarm. "I'm sure they just took a longer ride than anticipated."

"Can ye take some of yer men out for a search?" Elizabeth asked. "Something is wrong ... I sense it."

Cassian frowned. However, he didn't question her. Instead, he nodded and stepped out of the stall, heading toward the door. "I'll gather some of the Guard now."

Heart pounding, Elizabeth followed the captain outdoors, back into the snow.

She nearly ran into Cassian's broad back, for he'd abruptly halted a few feet outside the stable door.

Following his gaze, her own narrowing as she peered through the swirling snow, Elizabeth saw a horse ride in through the gate, leading a pony behind it.

"There he is." The relief in Cassian's voice was palpable.

However, Elizabeth was already rushing forward.

Even in the gloom, she could see that the garron was riderless. Where was Robbie?

As she neared the approaching outline of a tall man on horseback, Elizabeth saw that he carried a small figure in front of him—a figure that was slumped unconscious against his father's chest.

Terror twisted in Elizabeth's chest, and she broke into a run. "Robbie!"

XI

PROTECTIVE

ELIZABETH HURRIED TO Robert's side, her gaze spearing his for an instant, before it traveled down to Robbie's ashen face.

His eyes were closed, and only the rise and fall of his chest reassured her that her son was actually breathing.

"What happened?" The question came out in a panicked gasp. "Ye should have been home hours ago."

"Robbie's garron bolted on the way back from the woods," Robert answered, his voice rough with exhaustion. "The beast then threw him, but his foot caught in a stirrup, and he was dragged a good distance."

Elizabeth gasped, a hand rising to her mouth. "How seriously is he hurt?"

"He hit his head ... and I think he twisted an ankle badly."

"We must get him down off this horse and inside," Elizabeth replied, panic pulsing in her breast, in time with her heartbeat. She was aware that her voice sounded shrill—but she didn't care.

Robert only had one task today—to take his son out and ensure he didn't come to any harm.

He'd failed miserably.

"Elizabeth," Robert began, his voice strained. "I—"

"Help me get him down, Captain," Elizabeth called to Cassian, who was now striding toward them. "Robbie is injured."

She'd cut her husband off, but she didn't care. All she could focus on right now was Robbie.

Gently, Robert lowered Robbie's prone body down into Cassian's waiting arms. "Take him to my chamber, Captain," he said softly.

"No," Elizabeth interjected, not looking at her husband. "Take him to mine."

Cassian tensed, his gaze flicking between the laird and his wife. Robert didn't speak up and so, jaw tensing, Cassian nodded.

"Lady Elizabeth!"

A woman's voice echoed through the snowy gloaming.

Elizabeth swiveled to see Aila emerge, snowflakes settling on her hair. "The bairn is close now ... Gavina is calling for ye."

Elizabeth clenched her fists at her sides, frustration exploding within her. She was torn between tending to her son and assisting her friend. However, she knew Gavina needed her help with the birth, so she chose the latter.

Turning back to Cassian, she fixed him with a desperate look. "Make sure Robbie is kept warm and dry ... and I'll be down to see him as soon as I'm able."

"Elizabeth," Robert spoke up once more. "Don't worry, I'll look after him."

She forced herself to look at him then. Her husband's lean face was pale and strained, his eyes dark in the flickering torchlight. He looked worried—and so he should when he brought his son home half-dead.

"Like ye have done already?" Once again, she heard the sharp edge to her voice.

Robert's gaze widened, his bearded jaw growing taut, but Elizabeth didn't linger to hear his response. Instead, she turned and hurried after Aila.

Rosa Vulcan was born in the wee hours of the 'Long Night'.

A small wailing babe with a surprisingly full head of dark hair, the bairn's red face scrunched up in outrage.

"Someone has a fine set of lungs," Elizabeth noted with a weary smile. "Ye have a feisty lass on yer hands."

She wrapped the wailing bairn up in a soft cloth and handed her to Gavina.

Propped up on a mountain of pillows, her face pale with exhaustion yet glowing with pride, Gavina eagerly took the babe, holding it against her breast. "Rosa," she whispered. "My goodness ... ye are the very image of yer Da."

"Speaking of which ... I know someone who is very anxious to see ye both." Elizabeth moved over to the door and opened it, waving to the man who'd been pacing outside for hours. "Come in Draco ... ye have a bonny daughter."

Draco approached, his face still taut with worry.

"Fear not," Elizabeth murmured. "Both mother and bairn are well."

Her words were a balm to the man—almost instantly, she watched the tension ebb from him. Like Cassian, the first signs of age were on Draco these days. Not much, just the deepening of laugh lines around his eyes, mouth, and nose, and the barest hint of silver at his temples.

Draco Vulcan—like his friends Maximus and Cassian—had once been immortal, cursed by a Pict witch back in the mists of time. But seven years earlier he'd broken the curse, and now could age and die just like any other man.

Elizabeth stepped back to let him enter the chamber. Draco approached the bed and perched upon the edge, his hand reaching for his wife's. "Finally, a daughter," he murmured. "A lass for our boys to protect." He paused there, his gaze resting upon the babe's face. "She's beautiful," he whispered. "Like ye."

"Elizabeth and I both agree she looks like ye," Gavina replied, smiling up at him.

"Poor lass."

"Nonsense ... she will be a striking beauty, with many suitors vying for her hand."

"Not too many I hope," Draco growled. He continued to stare down at his daughter's wrinkled face—and the look of awe that Elizabeth saw there made her vision blur as tears rose.

He looked like the happiest man alive.

The castle slumbered when Elizabeth finally made her way down to her chambers.

The rest of the keep would have celebrated this eve by lighting the great oaken log in the hearth of the hall, and by enjoying a spread of seasonal treats washed down by mulled wine and mead.

Elizabeth hadn't eaten anything since noon—and hadn't any appetite now either.

It had been a privilege to deliver Gavina and Draco's daughter, yet it had been difficult to focus on the task—for her thoughts kept going to Robbie.

She needed to know how serious his injuries were.

Letting herself into the solar, she spied a tray of small pies and a cup of what smelled like mulled wine upon the table. However, she ignored the food and drink. Instead, she made her way across to her bed-chamber and opened the door.

Two figures lay upon the bed.

Elizabeth drew close, her gaze going to her son. He was wrapped up under a nest of blankets. Relief flooded through her when she saw—in the glow of the nearby hearth—that color had returned to his cheeks.

Reaching out, she lay a hand upon his brow. Warm, but not overly hot. She noted his breathing was slow, deep, and even—another good sign.

Reluctantly then, she shifted her attention to the second individual. Robert lay fully clothed on top of the bed, one arm slung protectively over his son's torso.

Protective.

Elizabeth's throat constricted, and she swallowed hard.

It was all well and good being caring now, when their son had almost met his end.

Even so—and although she bristled at the sight of her husband—her gaze took him in nonetheless. Robert looked exhausted, even sleep hadn't taken the tension from his face, or removed the dark smudges from under his eyes.

"Robert," she murmured, grasping him gently by the wrist. "Wake up."

Robert's eyelashes fluttered, and his eyes opened ... his gaze fixed upon her. "Liz?" His voice was gentle, husky—drawing her in.

Elizabeth fought the sensation. "Aye ... I'm back now, so ye can return to yer own chamber."

Robert removed his arm from over his sleeping son and sat up, running a tired hand over his face. "Hades ... my head feels full of wool ... what time is it?"

"Well after the witching hour." Elizabeth replied coolly. "Gavina and Draco have a daughter. Most folk are sleeping in their own beds, and so should ye."

He looked at her then, his gaze settling upon her with a gravity that made Elizabeth tense. "Ye are still angry with me?"

"Aye," she replied, not bothering to evade such a direct question.

"Ye think the accident my fault?"

"Well, isn't it?"

He stared back at her, his silence condemning him. "I do blame myself." he said after a few moments. "But it all happened so fast. Hunter had bolted before I could catch him by the reins."

"Ye should have kept a closer eye on Robbie," Elizabeth countered. Her belly clenched as anger spiraled up within her. "Ye treat him like a man, but he's only a lad ... ye were supposed to look after him."

"And I failed." Robert's voice was toneless as he finished Elizabeth's sentence for her. "Is that what ye are saying?"

He rolled off the bed and rose to his feet. Moving around the edge of the bed, he stopped before her.

Elizabeth raised her chin to hold his gaze, even if misery now clutched at her breast. She wanted to lash out, to wound. "Robbie's all I have," she eventually managed. "I'd never have forgiven ye if he'd broken his neck out there today. *Never.*"

Robert stared down at her, and long moments drew out. And as they did, she watched his brown eyes shutter.

A shield raised between them.

When Robert finally replied, his voice was as chill as the night that surrounded them. "Goodnight then, Liz," he said, before he moved past her and made for the door.

XII

IN THE STABLES

"YE WERE LUCKY, Robbie … it's only a bad sprain." Elizabeth finished wrapping the bandage around her son's swollen ankle before straightening up. She met his guileless brown gaze. "It could have been so much worse."

"Da saved me though," Robbie replied. He sat up in bed, his fingers wrapped around a fresh bannock smeared with butter and honey. "He stopped Hunter before he took us both over the cliffs."

Elizabeth's heart buckled against her ribs.

Robert didn't tell me that?

"God's teeth, Robbie … ye could have died."

Something in her tone made him stiffen, his eyes widening. "Are ye cross with me, Ma?"

Elizabeth straightened up from wrapping the bandage, meeting his eye. "No … why would I be?"

"Da said I shouldn't have fed Hunter all those oats … especially since he's cooped up inside with the snow."

Elizabeth inclined her head. "Excuse me?"

"Didn't Da say?" The lad's cheeks flushed as he realized he'd been caught out.

"No," Elizabeth replied slowly, before a sigh gusted out of her. "Why would ye do something so foolish, love?"

She was trying to keep the frustration out of her voice, but it was difficult.

"Hunter's such a slug." Robbie replied with a grimace. "I didn't want him to embarrass me, especially with Da."

"Robert wouldn't have cared."

"I want him to be proud of me ... I want him to think I'm as capable as he is."

"But ye are still a bairn," Elizabeth perched on the bed next to her son. "No one expects that of ye."

"I'm not a bairn." Robbie's jaw set in a stubborn expression she'd begun to see often of late. "Da says I'm almost a man."

Elizabeth stared down at her son, the desire to argue with him warring with the urge to chastise him. He was a headstrong lad—which was hardly surprising considering she and Robert were his parents.

At ten winters, he was still two or three years off making the transition from boy to youth—and like all lads, that day couldn't come soon enough.

"Ye have all yer life before ye, Robbie," she said after a pause, choosing her words carefully. "Don't wish these years away."

Her son held her gaze, and she could see he didn't fully comprehend her meaning.

"Ye will one day be laird of Dunnottar," she continued, reaching out and taking his hand. "Great responsibility will rest upon yer shoulders ... but for now, ye are young ... and carefree. Try to make the most of it."

Robbie cocked his head. "Didn't ye like being laird ... doesn't Da?"

Elizabeth smiled. "It's a privilege to rule a castle like Dunnottar ... but when the lives of many become yer responsibility, ye must weigh every decision carefully. Sometimes ye have to make yerself unpopular for the greater good ... it isn't always an easy mantle to bear." She squeezed her son's hand then, aware that she was becoming melancholy. "But ye don't need to worry about such things ... ye won't need to take on the role for a while yet."

Robbie watched her, and in his face, she saw her own inquisitiveness, her own desire for answers.

He really was a blend of the two of them.

"It's Da ye are truly angry with, isn't it?" Robbie said after a pause. "Ye hardly said a word to him when he visited me again at dawn."

"I was focused on ye," Elizabeth lied. She rose to her feet and started collecting up the bandages and clay bottles of unguents, placing them into her healer's basket.

"But ye wouldn't even glance at him." Robbie pressed, clearly not finished with the subject. "I saw the look on his face afterward. He seemed ... sad."

Elizabeth's chin jerked up.

Her son's words, untutored and instinctive, were like a punch to the belly.

Sad?

Robbie favored her with a sheepish smile then. "It wasn't his fault, Ma."

Robert didn't feel like celebrating Yule. The morning was bright and crisp, the snow a white veil over the hills around Dunnottar. The scent of roasting meat drifted through the keep, as did the sweet aroma of baking honey cakes—it was the smell of Yule, and at noon the folk of the keep would gather in the hall, under the garlands of ivy and mistletoe, to feast.

But Robert really wasn't in the mood to join them.

After checking on Robbie, and weathering his wife's cold shoulder, he'd gone out to the stables to look in on his courser and the errant Hunter. The pony was perfectly docile now, favoring him with a gentle nudge as he ducked into the stall.

"Morning, Trouble," he murmured, scratching the garron behind the ears. "I hope ye are going to behave yerself from now on."

The pony gave a snort in response. Picking up a coarse brush, Robert swept it over the garron's thick winter coat. The beast didn't really need grooming, but the action helped settle his mood, helped distract him from his own thoughts.

He would need to have words with Elizabeth at some point—although he wasn't looking forward to it.

She'd looked at him as if he were the devil last night when he'd brought Robbie home injured. And this morning, she wouldn't even meet his eye.

"Women," he muttered, letting out his frustration as he continued to brush Hunter. "Do ye understand them, lad? I certainly don't."

He'd been sure he and Elizabeth had turned a corner the night previous. They'd spoken honestly and even lain together, and he'd finally felt as if he'd come home.

But now he was out in the cold again—literally.

Elizabeth made it plain where her true affections lay. Her son was her world, and he couldn't really blame her for that. He'd been away for so long that Robbie had somehow taken his place in Elizabeth's heart.

And now she thought he'd deliberately put their son in harm's way.

I must tell her that it wasn't the case.

He'd tried last night, but her icy stare had made the excuses die upon his lips, had made anger rise within him. Anything he might have said would have likely been twisted against him—and so he'd held his tongue.

Loneliness swept over him then, dousing any lingering resentment toward his wife, in a cold cloak that chilled him to the marrow despite that the air was relatively warm inside the stables. It wasn't a new sensation—he'd weathered it for many years, but had thought he'd escaped it now he was home. Once again, he felt like an interloper. He was intruding on the life Elizabeth had built without him.

"Rob."

He glanced up then as a woman's voice cut through his brooding. Turning, he saw Elizabeth approaching, a fur mantle wrapped about her shoulders, her gaze fixed upon him.

"Liz," he greeted her gruffly. "What are ye doing out here?"

"Looking for ye."

He raised a questioning eyebrow. After the look she'd given him the last time he'd seen her, he'd imagined she'd wanted him to hurl himself from the walls. He hadn't expected her to seek him out.

"Why didn't ye tell me ye stopped Robbie's pony from taking him over the cliff?" she asked.

Robert turned properly to face her. "Ye didn't give me the chance."

Her cheeks reddened then, for he hadn't bothered to hide the note of chagrin in his voice.

"The lad fed the pony too many oats and then wondered why he couldn't control him properly." Robert continued when the silence between them drew out. "Hunter fought Robbie the whole way to the woods ... but on the way home, he took the bit between his teeth and bolted."

He cast a dark look over his shoulder at the pony, which was now innocently munching a mouthful of hay. When he glanced back at his wife, he saw that Elizabeth had drawn closer, her midnight-blue eyes—eyes he could drown in—wide and glittering.

"I'm sorry I jumped to conclusions," she murmured, her voice husky. "It's just that ...." Her voice died away as she struggled to explain herself.

Robert ducked out of the stall, rising to his full height before her.

"Ye don't trust me fully yet, do ye?" he asked. His tone was gentle although hurt twisted within him as he asked the question.

Her throat bobbed, betraying the truth. "I want to," she whispered. "It's just that for so long, it's only been Robbie and me ... I'm not used to sharing him with anyone." She swallowed hard and favored him with a rueful smile. "I'm afraid I'll never be a match for his father."

"Nonsense." Robert moved closer to her, a little of the tension he'd carried in his gut all morning loosening. "Ye are his mother ... no one can ever compete with that."

"Aye, but it's ye the lad admires," she huffed a brittle laugh. "The lad would follow ye through the gates of Hell if ye asked it." She broke off there, her gaze lowering.

"Liz?" Robert stepped up to her and reached out, his hands cupping her cheeks and raising her face so that their gazes met once more.

Her eyes brimmed with tears now. "And so would I, Rob," she whispered.

A tear escaped, and he brushed it away with the pad of his thumb. "Don't weep, my love," he whispered. "Do ye really think a wee misunderstanding between us would change how I feel about ye?"

"I don't know," she admitted softly.

He heaved in a deep breath. "Even after all these years apart, ye still know me better than anyone ... and ye always will. I love ye, Liz." The admission rushed out of him—and with it went the last remnants of tension. "This absence has only made what I feel for ye stronger. We have something that was made to last, mo chridhe ... please remember that."

She stared up at him, tears trickling down her cheeks. "And I love ye," she whispered, "so much that it hurts to breathe." A beat pulsed between them before she stretched up to him, her lips pressing against his.

An instant later, Robert's arms went around her and he crushed her against him, his mouth claiming hers.

EPILOGUE

LIGHT IN THE DARKNESS

ELIZABETH TOOK HER place near the head of the table, to her husband's left—and let the warm glow of contentment flow through her.

This was what she'd missed for so long—the sight of her husband seated in his carven chair at the head of the table.

Robert De Keith, laird of Dunnottar.

Reaching under the table, she placed a hand upon his knee.

Robert's gaze swiveled to her, a smile stretching across his handsome face.

Then, wordlessly, he placed a hand over hers. The warmth and strength of his hand made her breathing quicken, bringing her back to the stables, where he'd kissed her until they'd both been gasping for breath.

Servants appeared at the laird's table then, bringing in platters of roasted venison and goose stuffed with chestnut.

Elizabeth held up her silver, gem-studded goblet to be filled with dark-red bramble wine, while her gaze traveled around the hall. They'd made a fine job of the decorations this year—the scent of pine from the boughs they'd hung over the fireplace perfumed the air, and the garlands of green and red gave the hall a festive air.

Like most folk here, Elizabeth had dressed in her finest clothes: a crimson kirtle and surcoat trimmed in snowy ermine. Next to her, Robert also wore a surcoat trimmed in ermine, the white contrasting with his rich brown hair.

Around them, the rumble of voices blended with the gentle lilt of a harp.

Elizabeth took it all in—her chest aching as tears threatened. She wasn't a woman who wept at the slightest provocation, yet she had to blink rapidly to keep the tears at bay now.

They were tears of happiness.

Robbie hadn't joined them for the Yuletide banquet unfortunately. Instead, he would eat his meal propped up in bed. Likewise, Gavina, Draco, and their brood were absent from the table.

They would have a quiet celebration at Gavina's bedside.

But Cassian and Aila had joined the laird today—their two lads perched upon their knees, small hands reaching for pieces of venison. Aila wore a lovely emerald-green kirtle that contrasted with her creamy skin and walnut colored hair.

Farther down the table, Elizabeth spied Heather and Maximus and their two daughters. Pink-cheeked from the glow of the hearth, Heather looked as bonny as ever. She laughed then over something her husband had just said, her grey-green eyes twinkling. Beside her, Maximus Cato cut a striking figure, a wolfskin pelt wrapped around his broad shoulders. Silver now sprinkled the temples of his dark hair.

It warmed Elizabeth to know that her three best friends—Gavina, Aila, and Heather—had found happiness with their centurions. Three men who'd been cursed to an immortal life, but were now free to live and die like everyone else. The curse had also prevented them from fathering children, but these days all three were proud fathers.

I wonder what Robert would say if I told him about the curse. Elizabeth thought idly as she helped herself to some mashed, buttered turnip. Likely, he'd think she'd gone mad.

If she hadn't seen Cassian Gaius virtually rise from the dead seven years ago, she wouldn't have believed it either.

No, their story wouldn't be shared. This would be one secret she would keep. Robert would never learn the origin of these enigmatic three men who served him.

"Ye look pensive, my love." Robert's voice drew her gaze then, and she glanced right to find him watching her. "Does something worry ye?"

Elizabeth smiled. "Not anymore," she murmured. "I was just thinking how fortunate I am ... how grateful ... that ye returned to me." She raised her goblet to him then. "This keep never felt right with ye gone, Rob."

He smiled back and raised his own goblet, toasting her.

They both took a sip, their gazes fused as around them, laughter and merry voices rose and fell.

"And it still wouldn't feel right ... without the woman I love at my side," he replied. "Ye are what kept me going all those years, Liz." His hand, still clasped over hers on his knee, tightened. "There were times when I lost sight of it ... but somehow ye were always there ... the light in the darkness ... drawing me home."

FROM THE AUTHOR

I hope you enjoyed THE LAIRD'S RETURN. When I embarked on THE IMMORTAL HIGHLAND SERIES, I knew I wanted to tell Elizabeth and Robert's story—and since I'm a sucker for second chance love, I was really looking forward to it.

Elizabeth and Robert were once madly in love, but eight years apart have turned them into strangers. I enjoyed exploring their family dynamic and the barriers between two people who have both changed dramatically in their time apart, even though their love had never faded.

I didn't make Robert and Elizabeth up—they were real historical people. Robert De Keith II, laird of Dunnottar, wed Elizabeth Strachan, and they had a son (also called Robert). Their son went on to marry Elizabeth, the daughter of Scottish baron John Comyn.

Robert De Keith took up a military career as a young man, but was also considered by other Scottish barons to be a strong leader, being appointed justiciary of the lands beyond the River Forth. He was captured by the English in a skirmish near the River Cree in 1300, but was back in Scotland by 1308 (when this novella starts) and in March 1309 was present at Robert I of Scotland's first parliament at St Andrews. Robert commanded forces loyal to Robert Bruce at the Battle of Bannockburn.

I hope you enjoyed this novella. I love Christmas stories!

Jayne x

ABOUT THE AUTHOR

Award-winning author Jayne Castel writes epic Historical and Fantasy Romance. Her vibrant characters, richly researched historical settings and action-packed adventure romance transport readers to forgotten times and imaginary worlds.

Jayne is the author of the Amazon bestselling BRIDES OF SKYE series—a Medieval Scottish Romance trilogy about three strong-willed sisters and the men who love them. An exciting spin-off series set in the same story-world, THE SISTERS OF KILBRIDE, is now available as well. In love with all things Scottish, Jayne also writes romances set in Dark Ages Scotland ... sexy Pict warriors anyone?

When she's not writing, Jayne is reading (and re-reading) her favorite authors, cooking Italian feasts, and taking her dog, Juno, for walks. She lives in New Zealand's beautiful South Island.

Connect with Jayne online:
www.jaynecastel.com
www.facebook.com/JayneCastelRomance/
Email: contact@jaynecastel.com

Printed in Great Britain
by Amazon

11167525R00055